W9-DIZ-824

11/96

FIELD TRIP

Written and illustrated by Bob Reese

CHILDRENS PRESS®

CHICAGO

Thanks to my wife, Nancy, for her ideas and help in writing "School Days." A special thanks also to Fran Dyra for her inspiration and editing.

Library of Congress Cataloging-in-Publication Data

Reese, Bob.
    Field trip / written and illustrated by Bob Reese.
      p. cm. — (School days)
    Summary: A teacher and the ten children in her class
go on a field trip to a state fair.
    ISBN 0-516-05579-8
    [1. Schools—Fiction. 2. School field trips—Fiction.
3. Agricultural exhibitions—Fiction. 4. Stories in
rhyme.] I. Title. II. Series: Reese, Bob. School days.
PZ8.3.R255Fi 1992
[E]—dc20
                                             92-12186
                                                 CIP
                                                   AC

WELCOME TO
MISS NATALIE'S
CLASS-ROOM 21

Ten kids
line up.

4

Line up in pairs.

Field trip today.
We are going to the fair.

Field trip today.

We'll have a great time.

Field trip today.

Stay in line.

BEST PUMPKIN

Best pumpkin, . . . stay in line.

Best prize.
What a great time.

Pretty flowers, . . .

stay in line.

Big bull.
Oh, oh,
only nine.

Nine kids,
where is Liz?

Nine kids,
where is Liz?

Nine kids,
where is Liz?

The best prize.
There she is!

WORD LIST

a	have	pretty	today
are	in	prize	trip
best	is	pumpkin	up
big	kids	she	we
bull	line	stay	we'll
fair	Liz	ten	what
field	nine	the	where
flowers	oh	there	
going	only	time	
great	pairs	to	

About the Author

Bob Reese lives with his wife Nancy in the mountains of Utah with two dogs and five cats. They have two daughters, Natalie who is a resource teacher in Utah and Brittany who is studying to be a dancer in New York City.

Bob worked for Walt Disney and Hanna Barbera studios and has a BA degree in art and business.